The Biggest Birthday Cake in the World

Written by

Elizabeth Spurr

Illustrated by

Rosanne Litzinger

For Brinlee Brown,
Happy 5th
birthday!

Elizabeth Spurr
7/24/91

Harcourt Brace Jovanovich, Publishers

San Diego   New York   London

HBJ

Requests for permission to make copies of
any part of the work should be mailed to:
Permissions Department,
Harcourt Brace Jovanovich, Publishers,
Orlando, Florida 32887.

Library of Congress Cataloging-in-Publication Data
Spurr, Elizabeth.
The biggest birthday cake in the world/written by
Elizabeth Spurr; illustrated by Rosanne Litzinger.
p.   cm.
Summary: The richest and fattest man in the world
wishes for the biggest birthday cake in the world,
and on his birthday discovers the joy of sharing.
ISBN 0-15-207150-4
[1. Sharing—Fiction. 2. Cake—Fiction. 3. Birthdays—Fiction.]
I. Litzinger, Rosanne, ill. II. Title.
PZ7.S7695Bi   1991
[E]—dc20   89-19901

First edition
A B C D E

The illustrations in this book were done on Strathmore Bristol 3-ply paper,
using Winsor & Newton opaque watercolors and colored pencils.
The display type was set in Medici Script.
The text type was set in ITC Galliard.
Composition by Thompson Type, San Diego, California
Color separations were made by Bright Arts, Ltd., Singapore.
Printed and bound by Tien Wah Press, Singapore
Production supervision by Warren Wallerstein and Michele Green
Designed by Michael Farmer and Trina Stahl

For my children,
Matthew, Susan, Peter, Stephanie, Maureen
— E. S.

For M and D,
with love
— R. L.

I N THE OLD DAYS, when rich men were fat because they had enough to eat and poor men were thin because they didn't, the Richest Man in the World was, of course, the Fattest Man in the World.

The Richest-and-Fattest wore a dotted bow tie, eight diamond rings, and a cutaway coat (to give his stomach more room). He lived in the Biggest House in the World, all alone but for his staff: 100 cooks and three vice presidents.

Four weeks before he turned 40 years old, the Richest-and-Fattest called his staff to the great dining hall, where he spent most of his time. "September 31," he announced, "will be my birthday." (He was so rich, he had bought September 31, so no one else could use it.) "I would like to have the Biggest Birthday Cake in the World."

"Co-*los*-sal idea," said the first vice president.

"Stu-*pen*-dous," said the second.

"Ti-*tan*-ic!" said the third.

"I want chocolate," said the Richest-and-Fattest, with a glint of icing in his eyes, "mostly chocolate. Oozing with whipped cream and pudding. With pink sugar roses on top." He sighed and nodded his head, wobbling his 17 chins. "I'm not sure that I can wait!"

So the three vice presidents bought a bakery, where the 100 cooks
began to pour and sift, beat and stir. They cracked 40,000 eggs, mixed

them with 31,500 pounds of flour, 12,000 pounds of sugar, 7,000
pounds of cocoa, and 2,500 gallons of milk.

When the ovens were lit, the Sweetest Smell in the World began
floating from the bakery windows, making the children of the town,
oh, so hungry. They followed the scent from the bakery to the
railroad yard, where the 100 cooks were loading the cake onto

flatbed cars. When the train started moving, the children followed
the warm, moist aroma — over hills, under bridges, and through
tunnels — to a broad, grassy field.

The Richest-and-Fattest and his three vice presidents stood waiting beside a platform covered with seven acres of white linen. The 100 cooks looked like ants struggling with crumbs as they unloaded the layers, each a short block long.

"Mon-u-*men*-tal," said the first vice president.

"Pro-*di*-gious," said the second.

"Gar-*gan*-tu-an," said the third.

"Just the right size!" said the Richest-and-Fattest.

The children watched as the 100 cooks stacked the cake, like workmen erecting a building. They whirled the frosting in cement mixers, squirted it with hoses, and smoothed the chocolate with trowels. One cook, dangling from a construction crane, trimmed the cake with vanilla piping and pink sugar roses.

Every day the Longest Limousine in the World brought the three vice presidents and the Richest-and-Fattest to the field to supervise the work. "More peaks on the whipped cream," the Richest-and-Fattest would shout through his megaphone. "And move that rose a little to the right."

Each day after school the children came to watch the cake grow higher.

"We must do something about those children," said the Richest-and-Fattest. "They look hungry."

"*Rav*-en-ous," said the first vice president.

"Vo-*ra*-cious," said the second.

"Ra-*pa*-cious," said the third.

So the vice presidents roped off the cake and hired security police, who put up bold red and white signs:

HANDS OFF
KEEP OUT
NO CHILDREN ALLOWED

Saturday, September 31, came at last. The finished cake stood in splendor, like an ice-capped mountain in the morning sun. It cast a long shadow across the children who were gathered in wonder behind the rope. Inside the barrier the 100 cooks proudly surveyed their work.

When the vice presidents had tugged the Richest-and-Fattest from the car, they were greeted by a photographer from the local newspaper. "Let me get a picture of you welcoming your guests." He motioned toward the children.

"Guests? There are no guests," said the first vice president. "This party is very ex-*clu*-sive."

"Se-*lec*-tive," said the second.

"Pres-*ti*-gious," said the third, waving the children back.

"But who will eat the cake?" asked the photographer.

"*I* will," said the Richest-and-Fattest.

"All by yourself?"

"Why, yes. I'm quite sure I can eat it all," said the Richest-and-Fattest. His eyes twinkled at the thought. "Of course, it may take a day or two."

The three vice presidents looked at each other in amazement.

"*Glut*-ton-ous," whispered the first.

"Av-a-*ri*-cious," hissed the second.

"E-*da*-cious," mumbled the third, "and also downright piggish."

The 100 cooks said nothing. They hung their heads in disappointment, then slowly filed away.

Bowing to the photographer, the first vice president handed the Richest-and-Fattest a three-foot silver cake knife tied with a pink ribbon.

"Wait," said the second vice president. "First you must blow out the candles."

"With *this* cake," said the third vice president, "you can make the Biggest Wish in the World!"

The Richest-and-Fattest looked up to the 40 candles blazing in the breeze, each the size of a man. "Hmmm," he wheezed from behind his chins. "I think I'd like to wish for a rowboat. Ah, yes. That's what I've always wanted—one that won't sink when I get in."

"Pre-*pos*-ter-ous," said the first vice president.

"*Lu*-di-crous," said the second.

"Lu-*gu*-bri-ous," said the third.

"What *shall* I wish for, then?" asked the Richest-and-Fattest.

"Why, All the Money in the World, of course," said the first vice president.

"I already have enough money," said the Richest-and-Fattest.

"There is no such thing as enough money," said the second vice president.

"And if there is," said the third, "you can give what's left over to *us*."

The three vice presidents loaded the Richest-and-Fattest into a
large ballooning basket that hung from the construction crane.
He was hoisted up, up, up to the topmost layer.

The Richest-and-Fattest shut his eyes tight and said, "I wish for
All the Money in the World." He huffed and he puffed, but the
flame barely flickered. And there were 39 candles to go!

"Try again," called the three vice presidents. "Harder! Closer!"
The Richest-and-Fattest leaned out of the basket and blew until his face turned bright red. Nothing happened. He sank back into the basket, exhausted.

As he rested there, he heard the Sweetest Sound in the World: a few faint notes of music drifting up past the roses and candles. Peering down, he saw one tiny boy who, dressed in his Sunday suit, had walked under the barrier rope. The child was holding a large homemade card that said in crooked crayoned letters:

HAPPY BIRTHDAY

As the boy sang in a weak little voice, "Happy Birthday to You," the other children took up the song, joining hands and circling the cake.

As he listened, the Richest-and-Fattest felt something strange happen under his checkered vest. Deep inside he felt warm and squishy, like the center of a toasted marshmallow. A large teardrop rolled down his cheek and bounced onto a pink sugar rose, where it sparkled like dew.

"Thank you, thank you!" he called down to the children. "This *will* be a happy day."

One more time the Richest-and-Fattest tried to blow out
the candles, stretching way out over the rim of the basket. HUFF!
A strong gust of wind came from the clouds, snuffing out the
flames. It swung the basket through the air, tossing the Richest-
and-Fattest belly-side-down into the chocolate and cream.
SPLAT!

"Help me! Help me!" he wailed through a mouthful of fudge.
Sprawled like a turtle in a mire of chocolate mud, he could not get up.

The first vice president looked up at the flailing mess, then down to
his tidy striped trousers. "Help him," he called to the second
vice president.

"Help him," cried the second, ducking a shower of chocolate
pudding.

"Help him," shouted the third. He ran to put up the
limousine top.

"*We*'ll help you," chorused the children. They took the rope from the barrier and tossed it to the Richest-and-Fattest. Then, forming a line, they yanked with all their strength, until, finally, KABOOSH! The Richest-and-Fattest slid through the devil's food goo, bringing the whole top layer down with him.

"Thank you," he spluttered through the bittersweet and nuts. "Come, let's all enjoy!"

The children handed him the knife. "Not until you cut the cake and wish," they said. "That's the birthday rule."

This time the Richest-and-Fattest asked for something quite different. "I wish," he said through his milk-chocolate mask, "for All the Happiness in the World." He began to push on the knife.

"No!" He stopped. "I take that back. If *I* have all the happiness, there won't be any left for you, my friends." He turned toward the children. "I wish for happiness — but only my share."

The first huge slice fell PLOP! "Hooray!" shouted the children. When the 100 cooks heard the cheer, they came back to the party, tossing their puffy white hats in the air.

From then on no one used the knife. Led by the Richest-and-Fattest, boys, girls, and cooks dived into the cake, burrowing and tunneling, smudging and sludging, licking and sticking, making the Most Horrendous Mess in the World.

"In-*suf*-fer-a-ble!" said the first vice president.

"De-*spi*-ca-ble!" said the second.

"A-*bom*-i-na-ble!" said the third. He started the limousine engine, and the three vice presidents rolled away.

The children ate for hours, stuffing in as much as they could, somersaulting through the Most Heavenly Mush in the World, and laughing, "Har de har har haroo!"

But no one, of course, could "har de har" louder than the Richest-and-Fattest, Marshmallow-and-Chocolatest, Whipped-Creamiest, Happiest Man in the World.